MOTHER GOOSE
NURSERY RHYMES

RETOLD AND ILLUSTRATED BY
FRED CRUMP, JR.

TO SOW THE FALLOW SOIL

Winston-Derek Publishers, Inc.
Pennywell Drive—P.O. Box 90883
Nashville, TN 37209

First printing

PUBLISHED BY WINSTON-DEREK PUBLISHERS, INC.
Nashville, Tennessee 37205

Library of Congress Catalog Card No: 88-51224
ISBN: 1-55523-194-2

Printed in the United States of America

Mother Goose

Nursery Rhymes

MOTHER GOOSE
NURSERY RHYMES

Retold and Illustrated by

Fred Crump, Jr.

THIS BOOK
BELONGS TO

_____

LITTLE MISS MUFFET

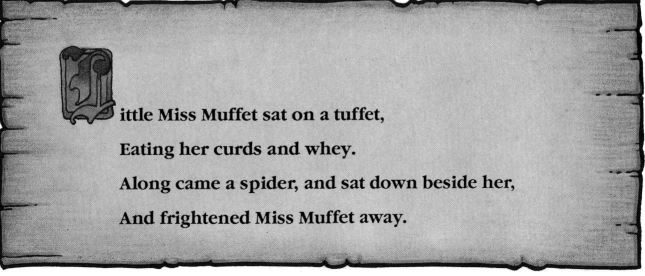

Little Miss Muffet sat on a tuffet,

Eating her curds and whey.

Along came a spider, and sat down beside her,

And frightened Miss Muffet away.

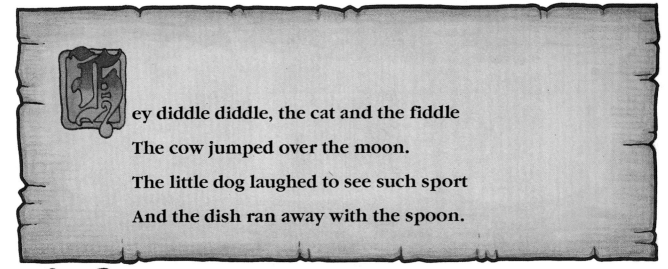

ey diddle diddle, the cat and the fiddle

The cow jumped over the moon.

The little dog laughed to see such sport

And the dish ran away with the spoon.

HEY DIDDLE DIDDLE

Old King Cole was a merry old soul,

And a merry old soul was he;

He called for his pipe and he called for his bowl

And he called for his fiddlers three.

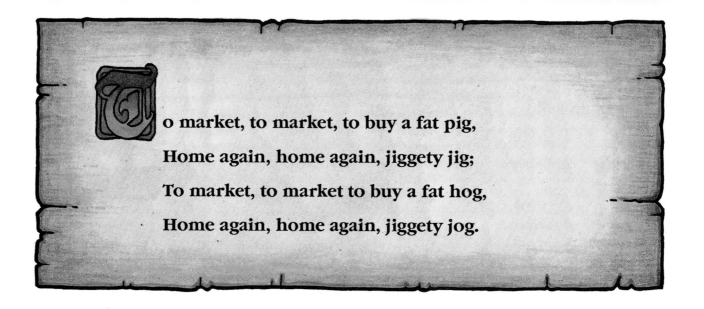

To market, to market, to buy a fat pig,

Home again, home again, jiggety jig;

To market, to market to buy a fat hog,

Home again, home again, jiggety jog.

Peter Piper picked a peck of pickled pepper;

A peck of pickled pepper Peter Piper picked;

If Peter Piper picked a peck of pickled pepper,

Where's the peck of pickled pepper Peter Piper picked?

Yankee Doodle went to town

Riding on a pony,

Stuck a feather in his hat,

And called it macaroni.

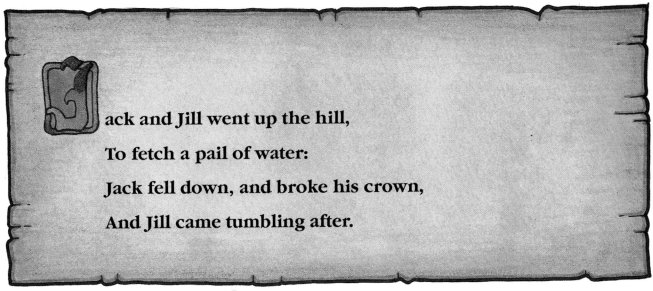

ack and Jill went up the hill,

To fetch a pail of water:

Jack fell down, and broke his crown,

And Jill came tumbling after.

JACK AND JILL

ittle Bo Peep has lost her sheep,

And doesn't know where to find them;

Leave them alone, and they'll come home,

Wagging their tails behind them.

LITTLE BO PEEP

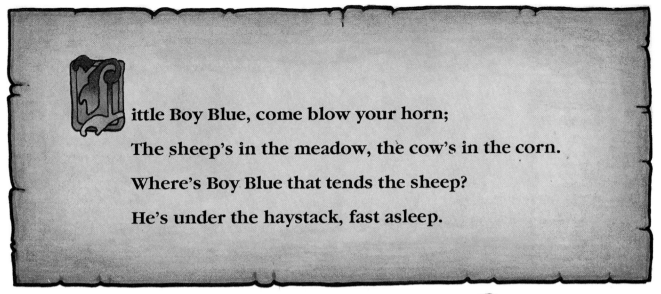

ittle Boy Blue, come blow your horn;

The sheep's in the meadow, the cow's in the corn.

Where's Boy Blue that tends the sheep?

He's under the haystack, fast asleep.

LiTTLE BOY BLUE

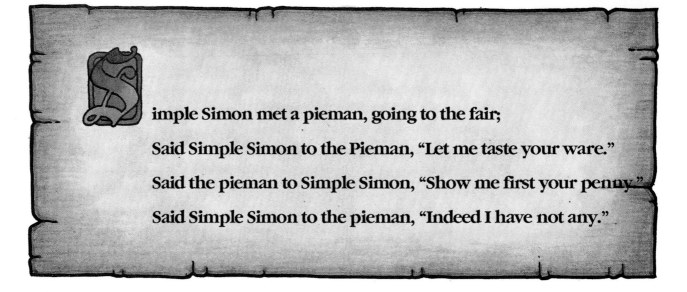

imple Simon met a pieman, going to the fair;

Said Simple Simon to the Pieman, "Let me taste your ware."

Said the pieman to Simple Simon, "Show me first your penny."

Said Simple Simon to the pieman, "Indeed I have not any."

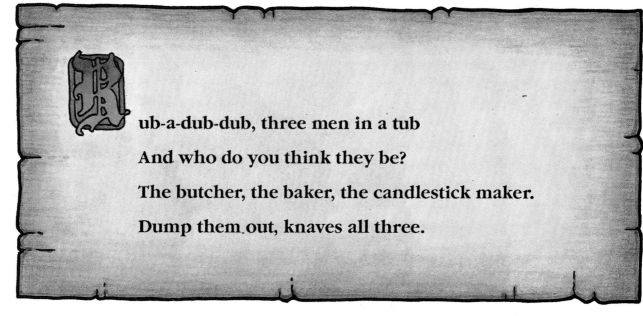

ub-a-dub-dub, three men in a tub

And who do you think they be?

The butcher, the baker, the candlestick maker.

Dump them out, knaves all three.

ary had a little lamb,

 Its fleece was white as snow;

And everywhere that Mary went

The lamb was sure to go.

Old Mother Hubbard went to the cupboard,

To fetch her poor dog a bone;

But when she got there the cupboard was bare

And so the poor dog had none.

OLD MOTHER HUBBARD

Hickory Dickory Dock

The mouse ran up the clock.

The clock struck one,

And down he run, Hickory Dickory Dock.

HICKORY DICKORY DOCK

PETER PETER PUMPKIN EATER

Peter, Peter, pumpkin-eater,

Had a wife and couldn't keep her:

He put her in a pumpkin shell,

And there he kept her very well.

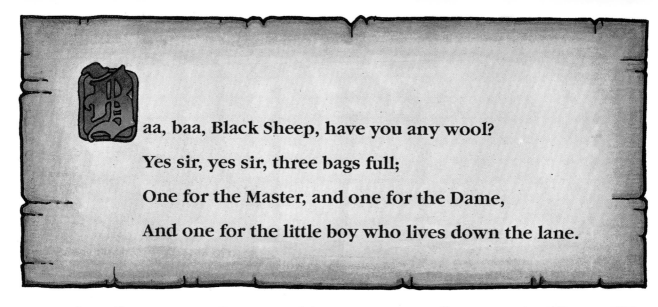

aa, baa, Black Sheep, have you any wool?

Yes sir, yes sir, three bags full;

One for the Master, and one for the Dame,

And one for the little boy who lives down the lane.

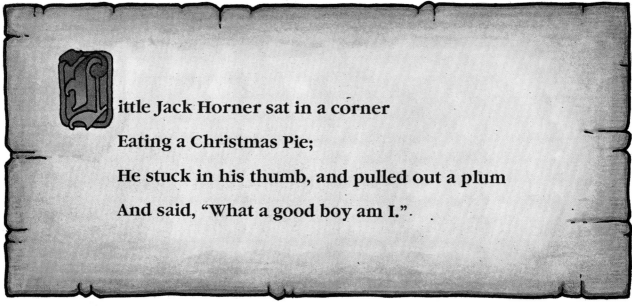

ittle Jack Horner sat in a corner

Eating a Christmas Pie;

He stuck in his thumb, and pulled out a plum

And said, "What a good boy am I."

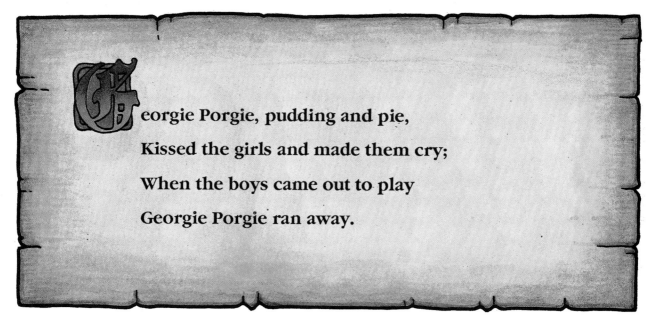

eorgie Porgie, pudding and pie,

Kissed the girls and made them cry;

When the boys came out to play

Georgie Porgie ran away.

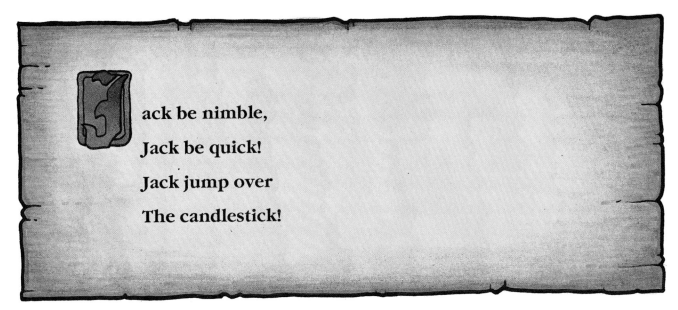

ack be nimble,

Jack be quick!

Jack jump over

The candlestick!

JACK BE NIMBLE

13

ack Sprat could eat no fat,

His wife could eat no lean;

And so between them both, you see,

They licked the platter clean.

JACK SPRAT

THREE LITTLE KITTENS

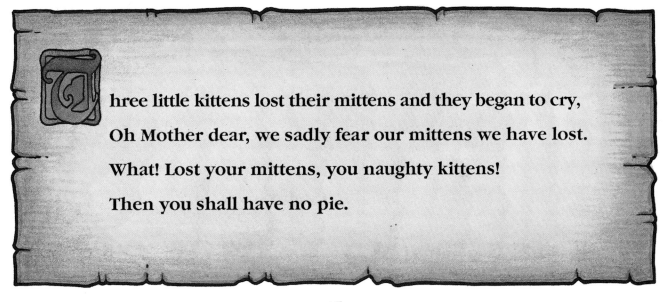

hree little kittens lost their mittens and they began to cry,

Oh Mother dear, we sadly fear our mittens we have lost.

What! Lost your mittens, you naughty kittens!

Then you shall have no pie.

Sing a song of sixpence, a pocket full of rye;

Four and twenty blackbirds baked in a pie.

When the pie was opened the birds began to sing;

Wasn't that a dainty dish to set before the king?

Roses are red,

Violets are blue,

Sugar is sweet

And so are you.

Pickety, Pickety, my black hen,

She lays eggs for gentlemen;

Gentlemen come every day

To see what my black hen does lay.

istress Mary, quite contrary,

How does your garden grow?

With blue bells and cockle shells

And pretty maids all in a row.

MISTRESS MARY, QUITE CONTRARY

here was an old woman who lived in a shoe;

She had so many children she didn't know what to do.

She gave them some soup, without any bread:

She spanked them all soundly and sent them to bed.

THERE WAS AN OLD WOMAN

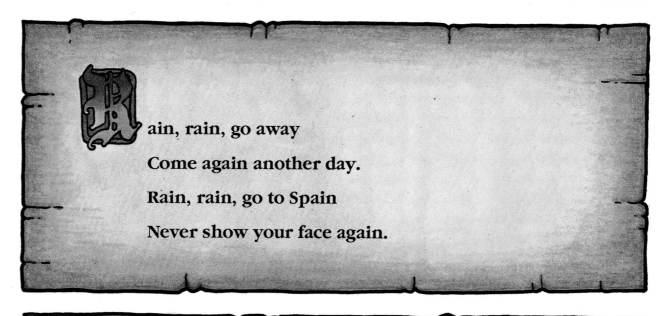

Rain, rain, go away
Come again another day.
Rain, rain, go to Spain
Never show your face again.

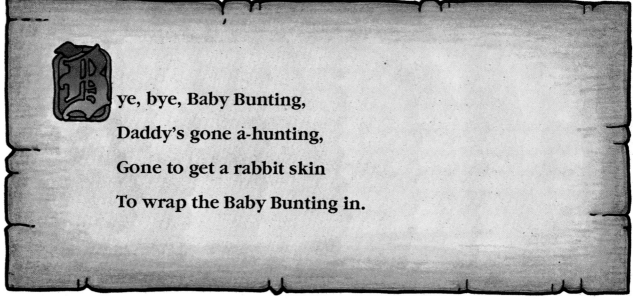

Bye, bye, Baby Bunting,
Daddy's gone a-hunting,
Gone to get a rabbit skin
To wrap the Baby Bunting in.

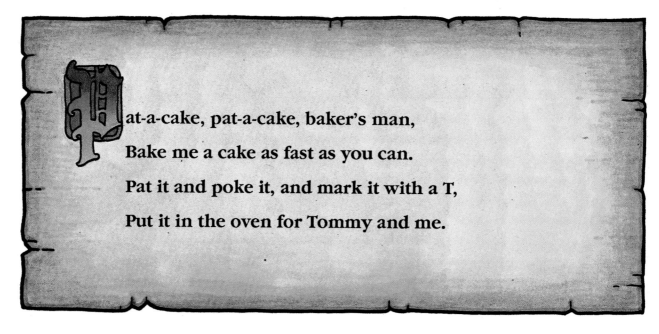

Pat-a-cake, pat-a-cake, baker's man,
Bake me a cake as fast as you can.
Pat it and poke it, and mark it with a T,
Put it in the oven for Tommy and me.

ITSY BITSY SPIDER

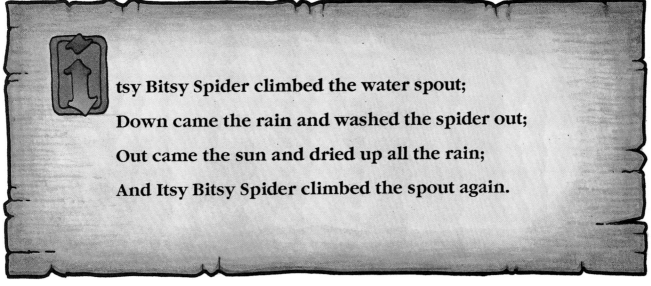

tsy Bitsy Spider climbed the water spout;

Down came the rain and washed the spider out;

Out came the sun and dried up all the rain;

And Itsy Bitsy Spider climbed the spout again.

THE QUEEN OF HEARTS

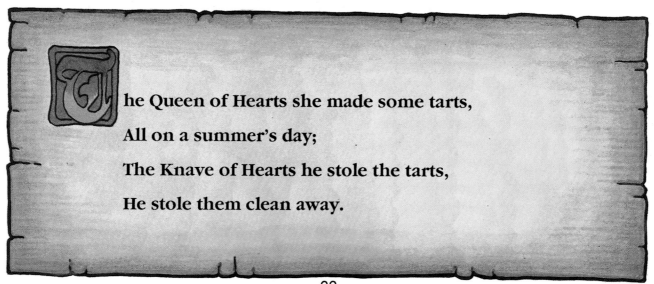

he Queen of Hearts she made some tarts,

All on a summer's day;

The Knave of Hearts he stole the tarts,

He stole them clean away.

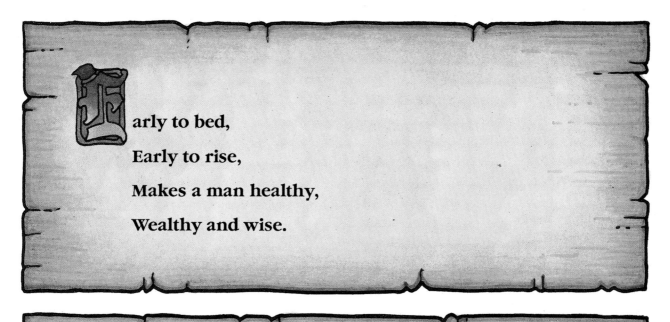

Early to bed,

Early to rise,

Makes a man healthy,

Wealthy and wise.

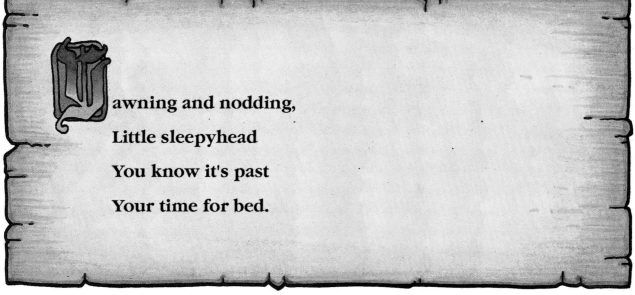

Yawning and nodding,

Little sleepyhead

You know it's past

Your time for bed.

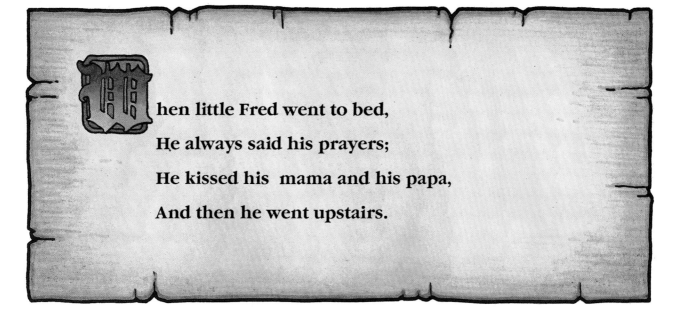

When little Fred went to bed,

He always said his prayers;

He kissed his mama and his papa,

And then he went upstairs.

umpty Dumpty sat on a wall,

Humpty Dumpty had a great fall:

HUMPTY DUMPTY

All the King's horses and all the King's men
Couldn't put Humpty together again.

I'm glad the sky is painted blue

And earth is painted green,

With such a lot of nice fresh air

All sandwiched in between.

Hippety hop to the barber shop,

To get a stick of candy.

One for you and one for me,

And one for sister Mandy.

Do you love me,

Or do you not?

You told me once,

But I forgot.

TWINKLE TWINKLE, LITTLE STAR

winkle, twinkle, little star,

How I wonder what you are.

Up above the world so high,

Like a diamond in the sky.

ow I lay me down to sleep,

I pray the Lord my soul to keep.

If I should die before I wake,

I pray the Lord my soul to take.

TRADITIONAL FAIRY TALES

Retold and Illustrated by
Fred Crump

Mgambo and the Tigers

Beauty and the Beast

Hakim and Grenita

Thumbelina

Mother Goose

Cinderella

A Rose for Zemira

Little Red Riding Hood

Sleeping Beauty

Jamako and the Beanstalk

Afrotina and the Three Bears

Rapunzel

Rumpelstiltskin

The Ebony Duckling

**A New Dimension in Fairy Tales for Children
Start Your Collection Today!**

CALL OR WRITE:

TO SOW THE FALLOW SOIL

Winston-Derek Publishers, Inc.
Pennywell Drive • P.O. Box 90883 • Nashville, Tennessee 37209 • 1-800-826-1888